Alexander Addison

An Oration on the Rise and Progress of the United States of America

to the present crisis, and on the duties of the citizens

Alexander Addison

An Oration on the Rise and Progress of the United States of America
to the present crisis, and on the duties of the citizens

ISBN/EAN: 9783337382322

Printed in Europe, USA, Canada, Australia, Japan

Cover: Foto ©Andreas Hilbeck / pixelio.de

More available books at **www.hansebooks.com**

AN

ORATION

ON THE

RISE AND PROGRESS

OF THE

UNITED STATES OF AMERICA,

TO THE

PRESENT CRISIS;

AND

ON THE DUTIES OF THE CITIZENS.

By ALEXANDER ADDISON, Esq.

Philadelphia:

PRINTED BY JOHN ORMROD, No. 41,

CHESNUT-STREET.

1798.

ORATION.

AFTER the peace of seventeen hundred and sixty-three, the British ministry proposed to raise a revenue by act of Parliament, from their American colonies. The sum, which, in this manner, they determined to raise, was indeed small, and not equal to the hazard of a revolution, or the expence of a war; but the people of America saw that a violation of principle ought to be resisted in the first instance, and at all hazards; and that, if they once yielded to extortion, there would be no end of demands; and if they once abandoned their right of self-government, there would be no restraint on oppression.

Resistance, war, and a revolution ensued. Providence countenanced the American cause, raised up to us allies among the rivals and enemies of Britain, and the colonies were acknowledged free and independent States.

But as waves long agitated by the wind do not subfide at the moment of the calm, the rancorous paffions excited by the revolution war were not foothed. by the peace of 1783; but reciprocally ftirred in the bofom of Britain and America. Concealed enmity, a delay of juftice, and alternate injury, were the confequences. The treaty of peace was not executed on either fide. *They* complained that they were not permitted to recover their debts. *We*, that we were not permitted to occupy our pofts. Thefe, ftill maintained by Britifh garrifons, prevented the fale and fettlement of an extenfive country, and if they did not excite and countenance, at leaft difabled us from fuppreffing, a pernicious and expenfive Indian war.

During all this time, America regarded France with a gratitude and affection approaching enthufiafm. France, next to the courage and perfeverance of the American people, was regarded as an inftrument under God of fecuring American independence. Yet France herfelf never pretended that fhe engaged in our conteft from any affection for liberty, or for the United States; but from hoftility to Britain and a defire to weaken this ancient enemy, by depriving her of the ample fource of commerce and wealth which the American colonies furnifhed.

It is thus that the Almighty in whofe hands are the hearts of kings and of all men, fometimes converts their worft paffions into inftruments of ufeful purpofes. The luft of Henry VIII. was made an inftrument of the reformation in England ; and the enmity of France againft Britain was made an inftrument of American independence.

The theories of philofophy and the practical leffons of the American revolution kindled a fire of liberty in France which foon blazed into a flame and confumed the fabric of her former government.

America viewed the commencement of the French revolution with fympathy and hope, and its progrefs with exultation and triumph. The caufe of France was confidered as the caufe of liberty—as our caufe. We excufed her outrages, we deplored her defeats, we rejoiced in her victories, as if they were all our own. She needed not, fhe declared that fhe did not defire the aid of our arms. But we made every exertion to fupply her and her colonies with provifions, in the moft feafonable and efficacious manner. We received her citizens with every mark of hofpitality. Our government in-ftantly, and firft of all the nations of the earth, acknowledged her as a Republic, and defying all chance of counter-revolution and the rifk of Bri-tifh refentment, paid to the agents of this republic, at a time of urgent neceffity, and before it was due, every dollar of our debt to the king. France can-not charge the people of America with want of gra-titude, nor the government of America with want of juftice.

Yet though the American government went to the utmoft extent of duty, by a punctual and a ge-nerous performance of her treaties and obligations, as France declared it to be her wifh, America knew it to be her intereft, by not overftepping the boun-dary of duty, to preferve herfelf from war. Ame-rica in the European war would have been but as a drop in the bucket, and her entering into it on the fide of France, would have increafed her debt, ruined her trade, and made her an ufelefs ally, and an impoverifhed and burdened nation. She could aid France better by neutrality than by being a party in the war.—Our government, therefore, and with profeffions of approbation from France, de-termined on a ftrict and impartial neutrality, and, while confiftently with neutrality, fhe honeftly and ufefully ferved France, adhered to this determina-tion with unimpeachable fincerity and perfeverance.

Ample proof has been made of this by Mr. Jeffer-
fon, in his letter for the recall of Mr. Genet.

But the profeffions and the purpofes of France
did not agree. Mr. Genet, the very minifter, who
on his arrival at Philadelphia, publicly declared,
that it was not the wifh nor intereft of France that
America fhould engage in the war, afterwards publifhed inftructions given him by the French government before his departure from France, enjoining
him to endeavour to engage America in the war
againft Britain. The inflexible prudence of the
Prefident precluded all hope of Mr. Genet's fuc-
ceeding with the government, in this fubject of his
inftructions. He had recourfe, therefore, to other
means. He fitted out privateers in our ports, he
commiffioned and engaged our citizens to enter on
board thofe privateers. Britifh fhips were taken
within our jurifdiction, and fold in our ports.
Clubs or focieties were, under his fuggeftions,
formed throughout the continent; to hang on the
fkirts of government, cenfure all its meafures and
weaken its authority, by rendering it fufpected, and
to roufe the paffions of the people, and prepare
them for a fubmiffion and even ardent devotion to
the will of France. The inevitable tendency of
the meafures of Mr. Genet to embroil us with Britain, engage us in the war, and thus make us dependent on France, is clearly expofed by Mr. Jef-

ferfon in the letter already referred to.—The meafures of Mr. Genet were purfued though lefs openly
with not lefs perfeverance by his fucceffors: and
it has been the conftant object of the minifters of
France to give to that government an influence in
this country, by dividing the people from our
administration, and turning the efforts of the people againft the efforts of the executive to fubject
our public counfels to the will of France, to maintain among the people an hoftile difpofition to
Britain, and, by gradual and indirect means compel our government into open war with that nation.

Though the prudent and active fpirit of the Prefident preferved us from the full effect of thofe
infidious machinations—an open war with Britain,
and a confequent dependence on France; yet thofe
machinations and the intemperate partiality and
zeal for France manifefted by the people, and by a
ftrong party in Congrefs, could not fail to draw on
us the fufpicion of Britain, that we could not long
refift thofe inducements to war, and fhould very
foon be actually engaged in it. France had,
with refpect to our trading fhips, very early in
the war, caft off any regard to the treaty of
commerce between her and America. Britain had
no commercial treaty with us, and was bound to
us in this refpect, only by the general law of nations.
Even this law both nations foon ceafed to regard.

France fet, and Britain followed the example, of making unjuftifiable fpoliations of our trade. What will not men do, when they have power without immediate controul! The fpoliations of Britain had amounted to a vaft fum, and threatened the ruin of our commerce; when meafures were propofed by thofe called the friends of France in Congrefs to check thofe fpoliations. An embargo was adopted, and afterwards (at the requeft of the French minifter, who wanted to fend fupplies to their Weft India iflands) was taken off. Commercial regulations, a fufpenfion of commerce with Britain, and a fequeftration of Britifh debts were propofed. Thofe members of Congrefs, who had approved the neutral meafures of the Prefident, and were defirous of preferving the United States in peace, confidered thofe meafures as neceffarily tending to war with Britain, and fome as being in fact a caufe of it. The Prefident feemed to have viewed them in the fame light, and determined firft to try whether a negociation would not obtain juftice. The friends of the meafures thus prevented declaimed againft a negociation under fuch circumftances, loudly extolled the force and fpirit of America, reprobated the bafenefs of national fubmiffion to injuftice, and declared, that there was no profpect of fuccefs in negociation unfupported by the propofed vigorous meafures. Thofe of the fame party in the Senate reprobated the appointment of the negociator. And pains were taken, that both he and the negociation fhould be confidered as odious and unfuccefsful.

All prophets, like Jonah, are angry, if their prophecy be not accomplifhed ; and their endeavours are feldom wanting to promote its accomplifhment. The profpect of a negociation with Britain feemed fatal to the hope of France and her agents here, of involving us in the war. Thofe in Congrefs whofe propofitions were thereby prevented, felt the chagrin of difappointment. Thus a vaft intereft was eftablifhed in the United States againft any treaty whatever with Britain. Even before the treaty was known, it was attacked by conjecture. No fooner was it known, than town-meetings affembled in the moft tumultuous manner, and without argument or deliberation condemned it. It was cenfured for faults which had no exiftence, and evils created by imagination. The treaty was oppofed in every ftage, and even after it became a law a ftrong party in the Houfe of Reprefentatives endeavoured to defeat it. But it triumphed over all oppofition, the pofts were furrendered, our claims for fpoliations were put in an equitable mode of adjuftment. And great progrefs has, in confequence, been made in adjufting and paying them.

· · For a long time after the treaty was ratified and publifhed, France made little if any objections to it; and if fhe made any they were fuggefted to her by her partizans among ourfelves. Had they been filent, fo would France have been. But it was evident, if the prophecies of menace and refentment uttered by the partizans of France here were not fulfilled, they would lofe all credit and confequence; our government would triumph; thofe popular leaders would fink into infignificance; the influence of France on this country would ceafe; our government would be reftored to its confidence and authority; and the United States become really independent.

. Inftigated therefore by their party here, and to preferve its hold on the people of this country, and keep them dependent, by weakening the adminiftration by a feparation of the people from it, the French government at laft complained that our treaty with Britain was injurious to France; of themfelves took upon them to new-model their treaty with us; and proceeded to new and exorbitant fpoliations on our commerce.

That their objections to the Britifh treaty, and all their objections to the conduct of our government were but pretexts, and that the true motive of their refentment was to maintain their influence in this country to ufe the people againft the government of the United States, and thereby fubject both to the will of France; muft be evident to every candid and intelligent man, who reads the French objections to the Britifh treaty, and to other parts of the conduct of our adminiftration, as ftated in Mr. Adet's letter to our fecretary of ftate; and compares it with that plain and fatisfactory anfwer to all thofe objections in the letter of the fecretary. It muft be ftill more evident from the critical time which Mr. Adet chofe to ftate thofe objections, and from his publifhing them to the people juft before the election of Electors of a Prefident of the United States, when one of the candidates for that ftation was fuppofed to be devoted to the interefts of France, and was zealoufly fupported by all their partizans and agents in this country.

To thofe who do not read, and to thofe who read without thinking, all argument on this head is vain. But to thofe who have confidered the treaty, the objections, and the anfwers, I may fafely appeal. And I challenge any man, to point out any part of the Britifh treaty which is injurious to France, or which gives to Britain any advantage, which as an independent and neutral nation, we had not a right to give. If this be the cafe, and that it is the cafe has been often proved, and may be confidently believed, they muft have a wretched opinion of the principles, moderation, and integrity of the French government, who can think the Britiſh treaty a cauſe of war by France againſt America. What! are we a ſovereign and independent nation, and have we not a right to make ſuch contracts as we pleaſe, harmleſs to other nations? are we yet in a ſtate of infancy, and our acts to be conſidered void, and grounds of chaſtiſement, unleſs approved by our guardians? Did we emancipate ourſelves from the dominion of Britain, only to ſubject ourſelves to the dominion of France? Are the United States independent, if they dare not make ſuch treaties as they pleaſe, conſiſtent with prior engagements, and the general law of nations? And is the ſpirit of 1776 ſo completely extinguiſhed in the American breaſt, that we ſhall now tamely ſubmit to encroachments which then we reſiſted and repelled? Tame conceſſions to unjuſt demands, like the beginnings of ſtrife, are, as the letting out of water: the dam once broken, an irreſiſtable flood will ruſh in, and overwhelm us.

But ſuppoſing the making of the Britiſh treaty a cauſe of war by France againſt America, a violation of it, or a refuſal to comply with it, would clearly have been a cauſe of war by Britain againſt America. Britain had her complaints as well as we, and having propoſed a reaſonable accommodation, if we refuſed to comply with it, had a right to employ force to compel us. This right would have been the fame, if no treaty had been made, but merely a demand and refufal to pay Britifh debts. We have not to confider now, only whether the Britifh treaty be the caufe of the refentment and aggreffions of France; but alfo, what would have been our condition if that treaty had not been made, or being made, had been broken, or not executed. We fhould then, probably, have had an Indian war on our frontiers, and a war with Britain at fea. It is not hard to determine whether that, or our prefent ftate, with all we can fear from France, be the greater evil. Suppofing an invafion of our country from either, France could indeed raife, but probably could not tranfport a greater army than Britain. But fuppofing, as perhaps is the cafe, an invafion not probable, and only a fea war; there is no comparifon between the naval power of Britain and that of France, perhaps and that of the world: and our danger would be in proportion to the power of our enemy. If we have incurred therefore a danger, by making the Britifh treaty, we have thereby efcaped a far greater danger; an Indian war, and a fea war with the greateft naval power in the world.

But there is another difference between the two cafes, a difference which by all who believe and regard a divine Providence will never be loft fight of.

In our difpute with France we are contending for principle, for juftice, and for our independent rights, and refifting oppreffion and unjuft dominion. In the difpute to have been feared with Britain, if we refufed a peaceable accommodation, we fhould have had to contend for injuftice and iniquity. In our difpute with France, we have a a good caufe; in that with Britain, we fhould have had a bad caufe. Courage, and, if we can truft in Providence, fuccefs, is in proportion to confcience.

But though the Britifh treaty furnifhed no juftification, it was ufed as a pretext, for drawing on us the anger and vengeance of France. This vengeance was thought neceffary, to give confequence to their party, and maintain their hold on the people againft the government of America. It was the only remaining mean of preventing the complete emancipation of the United States from the yoke of foreign influence.

At an important time to influence the election of a Prefident of the United States, Mr. Adet announced not only to the government, but to the people, the fufpenfion of his diplomatic powers in this country, accompanied with vehement but filly and groundlefs complaints againft the government of the United States. This menace failing to pro-

duce the intended effect, the election of Mr. Jef-
ferfon as Prefident, was foon followed by the grof-
feft injuries to our trade, the capture of our veffels,
on the moft frivolous and unjuftifiable pretexts ;
till the damages have amounted, it has been faid, to
thirty million of dollars. Payment was alfo refufed
of a large debt contracted by the agents of France
for provifions furnifhed on the credit of that government. And it became the avowed object of
France to compel the United States to an implicit
fubmiffion to her will, or to ruin them.

. To all thefe invafions of our rights, depredations of our property, machinations againft our
peace and independence, and intrigues to draw us
into the war, the French government had been encouraged by our minifter in France, a weak zea-
lot, fubfervient to their ambition and infolence.
He foftered their hope that the people of the
United States were ready to make a common caufe
with France, and would cheerfully fubmit to any invafion of their rights or fpoliations of their commerce, that would contribute to the fuccefs of that
caufe. He neglected, in fpite of the pofitive and
repeated inftructions of the Prefident, effectually to
remonftrate againft the violations of our treaty and
neutral rights, committed on our commerce by the
French fhips of war and privateers. He neglected
alfo, contrary to exprefs inftructions, to give to the

French government the neceffary explanations of our treaty with Britain, and point out the mifconceptions on which the prejudice of France againft it, and the conduct of our government generally were founded. And he not only encouraged but ftrongly recommended a loan of money, by the United States to France, which would have been a plain breach of neutrality, and an open taking part in the war, and, of courfe, a caufe of war againft us by all the enemies of France. By fpeculations in the French funds, he purchafed a princely palace in the vicinity of Paris. His houfe was a refort for all difcontented Americans, where they were inftructed by him not in refpect, but difaffection of their own government. At his table he read and mifreprefented our treaty with Britain. In his houfe he entertained the profligate and impious Paine, while he wrote his fcandalous letter to General Wafhington, and had it recited to him as it was compofed, for his amufement.—And, at a public entertainment, he retired, while the health of the Prefident was drank, and immediately after returned. When fuch was the treacherous conduct of our minifter, no wonder that the French government broke through all reftraints of decency or juftice to us, no wonder that the Prefident recalled him, and no wonder that the Directory parted with him with regret.

As the French government were thus feduced to a falfe confidence in the bafenefs and depravity of the American fpirit; neither need we wonder that the American people were fo long deluded by a falfe opinion of the virtue of France, and have only renounced that opinion, when it becomes too plain to be denied, that the French government have abandoned all regard to God, to government, to juftice, or to decency. Vaft and inceffant pains have been taken throughout this country, to miflead the underftanding and the judgment of the people. Pamphlets and newfpapers have been continually iffuing from the prefs, for the avowed purpofe of deftroying all truft in God, and all confidence in our government. No public character, not even the virtue of a Wafhington, nor religion itfelf, has efcaped abufe and defamation. Every act of the government has been cenfured and mifreprefented and even the motives and intentions of public officers have been perverted and miftated. Every thing done by our government has been reprefented as conftantly wrong, every thing done againft us by the French, or any other government under their influence, as conftantly right; till we have feemed more willing to obey a mandate of the French Direc-tory, than a folemn act of our own adminiftration.

Thofe notorioufly falfe ftatements of public tranf-actions have been fupported by many who having

more concern in the adminiftration, or being near
the fource of information might have known (if in
fact they did not know) better. Many of our members of Affembly and members of Congrefs not
only in converfations but in letters have taken the
utmoft pains to diffeminate fufpicions and ill opinions of the moft refpectable officers and neceffary
meafures of the adminiftration ; and have rendered
it impoffible for the citizens to know the truth, or
to form a right judgment of men or things.
Hence the opinions and duties of the citizens were
perverted. And, as the nature of man is prone
to believe flander, the authors of thofe mifreprefen-
tations became popular in proportion to their ma-
lignity, and influenced the opinions and elections of
the people.

Of all whom I have had an opportunity of ob-
ferving, the member of Congrefs from the adjoin-
ing diftrict has been the moft bufy and mifchievous.
With a reputation for candour, patriotifm and
truth, which gave to all his ftatements the confidence of authenticity, his letters have filled the
country with falfe opinions of the acts and officers
of government, and falfe vindications of every
thing done againft it. The falfehood and malig-
nity of many of his reprefentations have been dif-
covered, and, if he have any value of reputation,
he will now ceafe to promote difaffection to the re-

gular adminiſtration of public authority; or if he
ſhould perſiſt, the credit of his reports has ſo much
fallen, that they will be leſs injurious. But hitherto
they have had a pernicious influence on the judgment and conduct of the people of this country.
He has publiſhed them in newſpapers. He has
ſent under cover to poſtmaſters, whom he knew
diſpoſed to be organs of the propagation of his
opinions, his letters to his correſpondents open, for
the purpoſe of being read and publiſhed by thoſe
poſtmaſters. His letters have been very frequent,
and his correſpondents often of a ſort not ſuffi-
ciently qualified to detect or correct the error and
poiſon conveyed in them. The late meſſage of the
Preſident has been a complete confutation of ſome
of the moſt malignant parts of them. It becomes
every man to aid in expoſing them, in order to re-
ſtore the people who have been miſled by them, to
a right judgment and conduct, and preſerve the
country from the dangerous effects of their deluſion.

While the people of America were thus miſre-
preſented by our miniſter in France, and miſled by
the partizans of France here, and while prejudice
and falſe opinions of the American goveramenſ
were thus induſtriouſly ſuggeſted and cultivated,
both there and here; we need not recur to the Britiſh treaty, nor to any conduct of our adminiſtration, for the cauſes of the French aggreſſions on

America, for they may be accounted for from the nature of man and the general principles and conduct of the French government.

Power without reftraint or accountability feldom fails to be abufed in the hands of men. The French had triumphed over all their enemies and were elated with victory. It was the intereft of thofe who poffeffed the powers of government to keep the nation embroiled, in order to maintain their ftation and influence. Early in the French revolution they publicly declared that they were ready to unite with a party in any nation to change the form of their government. And this, whatever they might afterwards profefs, they inceffantly purfued, wherever they had opportunity. It was indifferent to them whether the government which they affifted the difaffected to deftroy was a monarchy or a republic, arbitrary or free. The point with them was to excite and fupport a party, promote confufion, and fo acquire influence, predominancy, and plunder. Flanders, Holland, Italy, Germany, Switzerland and Venice, are ample proofs of this fpirit. The plunder of the church, the banifhment and murder of their fellow citizens, the perpetual deftruction and fucceffion of parties, and above all the contempt and extinction of all principles of morality, humanity, and religion, fhew, that we need not look beyond their own character, for caufes of mifchief from the French government. Can we expect juſtice from men who deny it to each other? Will thoſe reſpect the rights of man,·who contemn the rights of God? Can we expect any decency or right from men with power in their hands, who deny a God and·a future ſtate?

It is not therefore in the Britiſh treaty, nor in any part of the conduct of our own government, but in the character of the French government, and in our own diviſions excited by the ſlander and abuſe of our public officers, and meaſures, that we are to look for the cauſes of the French aggreſſions. A love of plunder and univerſal domination is plainly ſeen in all the conduct of the French government. And the influence they had acquired here, and the fatal diviſion between the people and the government, which they and their partizans had ſo inceſſantly and ſuccefsfully promoted; ſhewed us to be weak, becauſe divided, and therefore defencelefs, and an eafy prey. An houſe divided againſt itſelf cannot ſtand. The French government might therefore freely indulge their paſſion for plunder and power, unrelentingly perſiſt in their violation of our rights, and ſpoliation of our commerce, and ſet our government at defiance; ſince they had a party among ourſelves of ſtrength and diſpoſition competent to defeat every purpoſe of the government, and render all its meaſures odious. ✗

Confident therefore in thefe means of defeating any exertion for maintaining our national fovereignty, and determined to reduce us to a ftate of fubmiffion and dependence, when a minifter was fent to Paris, who really would obferve the inftructions of the Prefident, and would not fubmit to be a tool of the Directory ; they refufed to receive him and even threatened him with imprifonment, unlefs he left their territory. He accordingly retired to Holland, and waited for inftructions from the Prefident, to direct his future conduct.

To have a juft feeling of this grofs indignity, let us fuppofe that the Britifh court had thus rejected Mr. Jay, obftinately rejected all communication of complaints for the injuries done us, and told him he muft leave the country or perhaps go to prifon : What would have been the indignation of America! And how would the cry of war have refounded from all the partifans of France, even from all fpirited Americans ! And, was not the rejection of Mr. Pinckney by the French, a greater indignity ? Is not indignity from a friend whom we have loved, and praifed, more grievous, than like treatment from a man whom we have hated and abufed ?

Yet the American government did not refent this indignity, but refrained from hoftility ; and the prefent Prefident determined to make one effort

D

more for reconciliation. And, to give it more fo-
lemnity, appointed three Envoys to the French Directory, to endeavour to obtain juſtice and peace,
by ſtipulating for compenſation for paſt, and ſecuri-
ty againſt future injuries ; in a new treaty ſettling
all the diſputed conſtructions of the former, and
fixing the terms of our future intercourſe with
France.

It has been admitted by the greateſt ſlanderers of
the Preſident, and even contrary to their own pre-
vious ſuſpicions and reports, that the inſtructions given by the Preſident to his Envoys have been the
moſt liberal and candid, that could have been juſti-
fiable.—They authorized the Envoys, if this were
deſired by the French, to modify the commercial
treaty with France, according to the principles of
the Britiſh treaty ; to give up our claim for enemies
property captured in veſſels of the United States ;
to ſtipulate for our accepting ſecurities payable at a
future time, inſtead of money, for our claims for
depredations on our commerce ; and even not to
inſiſt on ſatisfaction of our claims as an indiſpenſa-
ble condition of the propoſed treaty.

With full powers and ſuch liberal inſtructions,
the envoys arrived in Paris on the 4th of October
laſt, and the day following announced their arrival
and their miſſion to the miniſter of foreign affairs.

His fecretary gave information, that the Directory were exafperated at Parts of the Prefident's fpeech, that the negotiation would be conducted under the direction of this minifter, and they would have no audience of the Directory till it was finifhed. Two weeks after their arrival, authorized and acknow-ledged agents of this minifter commenced conver-fations, preparatory to the negotiation. They be-gan by ftating the pride of the Directory, their great offence at certain parts of the Prefident's fpeech, and the humiliating apologies, difavowals, repara-tions, and explanations, which would be required from the envoys. Thefe however, they fairly avow-ed to be only pretexts for the purpofe of obtaining, what was their real object, and without which, the envoys were told, that they could expect no treaty nor even a reception, nor permiffion to remain in Paris; money! that with or without thefe apolo-gies, &c. money muft be given. They muft, in the firft place, give to the minifter about 223,000 dollars, to be employed by him in gaining the good will of the Directory. They muft advance to the French government a fum equal to all the American claims againft France, and the French government would then pay the claimants, and they lay out the money again in fupplies to the French colonies. They muft purchafe from the French government Dutch debts to the amount of about fix millions of dollars, as fometimes ftated, and twelve million of

dollars as stated at other times, paying twenty shil-
lings in the pound, when in the market they were
hardly worth ten. All this was to be done without
any affurance, that a negociation would be fuccefsful, without any ftatement of terms, and perhaps
without even a fufpenfion of hoftilities. Thefe
terms the envoys pofitively rejected. Argument
and menace were exerted in vain, to produce a
compliance.—The wrath and power of the French
government was fet forth in ftrong terms. It was
ftated that the prefent Directors would probably not
be long in power, and a temporary compliance
might prevent a war. That we had to treat with
men who difregarded the juſtice of our claims, and
the reafoning with which we fupported them : that
they difregarded their own colonies, and confidered themfelves as invulnerable with refpect to us ;
that we would acquire an intereft among them only by a judicious application of money ; that nothing
was to be obtained there without money ; and that
all the neighbouring ftates had, in like manner,
been obliged to purchafe peace. That if we did
not, they would confifcate our property, and embargo our veffels and ravage our coafts ; that we
might look for the fate of Venice, to be parcelled
out, and bartered away ; or at leaft have the form
of our government changed, as that of Hamburgh
and Switzerland would foon be ; or partake of a
like ruin as was hanging over Portugal and England.

That France had lent us money, and we ought to shew the fame friendſhip. That they had intelligence from the United States, that if Mr. Burr and Mr. Madiſon had conſtituted the miſſion, the differences would have been accommodated. That the miniſter was preparing a memorial, to be ſent out to the United States, complaining of the envoys, as being unfriendly to an accommodation with France. That they had a party in America ſtrongly in their intereſt; and that the diplomatic ſkill of France, and the means which ſhe poſſeſſes in our country, are ſufficient to enable her, with the French party in America, to throw the blame of the rupture of the negotiations on the federaliſts.

To theſe propoſals the Envoys replied, that, tho' ſenſible of the power of France, they could never conſent to purchaſe peace by a ſurrender of their national independence. That ſubmiſſion to claims not founded in right, inſtead of procuring ſolid peace, would only invite a repetition of demands without end. That they expected to receive, and were prepared, in the ampleſt manner, to give juſtice; and would make any reaſonable ſacrifice for the ſake of peace. That they were anxious to avoid war; but if war forced itſelf upon them, the United States had nothing left, but to exert their means of ſelf-defence; and that thoſe means were ſufficient to preſerve them from ſubjection to any go-

vernment. That while we were ſtruggling for liberty, we had ſolicited from France a loan of money as a favour, had not extorted it by threats or
injuries, nor exacted it as a condition of doing juſtice, or forbearing hoſtility; and that France had
lent it in the time of our diſtreſs, of her own choice,
and in order to maim and depreſs a rival nation.
That France now ſtood in no need of money for her
own defence, and wanted it only to extend her con-
queſts over other nations.—And that our lending it
to France, while engaged in war for that purpoſe,
was becoming parties in the war; and taking part
in the war under the coercion of France was ſurren-
dering our independence. That it would not be ea-
ſy for the miniſter to perſuade the people of America, that the ſtatements made by their Envoys are
untrue; at any rate he might be aſſured, that the
fear of cenſure would not induce them to deſerve
it. They would act according to their own judgment; and truſted they ſhould be ſupported by the
great body of candid and honeſt men. And that
France miſcalculated on the parties in America;
for the extreme injuſtice offered to our country
would unite every man againſt her.

The lateſt diſpatches received from our Envoys,
dated 8th January laſt, announce new meaſures
tending to the utter deſtruction of our trade, and
inform us, that after a ſtay of three months there,

unnoticed and unacknowledged, they have no hope
of being received, or of accomplishing the object of
their miffion. All this the Prefident has announced
to Congrefs, with a declaration, that no profpect
remains of accommodating our differences with
France, without a furrender of the effential principles of our independence.

' The crifis to which the United States are now
brought, is one of the moft extraordinary to be
found in the hiftory of nations. A fovereign ftate
confcious of no offence is caufelefsly attacked by a
proud and potent nation, and on pretexts as various
as they are groundlefs, and every day fhifting and
multiplying, is fpoiled of property to a vaft amount,
and threatened with the utter extinction of her
trade and her means of defence. Defirous to
avoid war, and to live on good terms with her
fpoiler, fhe fends to him meffengers of peace, to
difcufs the caufes and effects of her fufferings, and
even to forgive all that is paft, on condition that fhe
may live fecurely in future. Thefe meffengers, the
fpoiler firft refufes to hear, drives from him, and
threatens with imprifonment.——They are fent
back. They are ftill not fuffered to unfold their
complaints, or the powers of their miffion. Frivolous grounds of complaint againft the fuffering
ftate are fabricated. Submiffions are required, on
purpofe to mark their degradation, and fhew how

far the fpoiler might proceed in his plunder and demands. Thofe fubmiffions are acknowledged to be mere pretexts for exacting further enormous fums of money, as bribes or loans, to men who profeffed no regard to juftice, and might foon be out of authority. When all thefe terms were to be complied with, it was poffible the meffengers might be admitted to ftate their complaints, and propofe terms of redrefs; but in the mean time the fpoiler would proceed in his acts of violence.

That when the colonies fent petitions for redrefs to Britain, they were received contemptuoufly, was not matter of great wonder; for they were held as in a ftate of rebellion. But that when one fovereign ftate, having received unexampled and unprovoked injuries from another, has fent ambaffadors to difcufs the grounds of injury, and means of redrefs, thofe ambaffadors are treated contemptuoufly, and difmiffed unheard; and are moreover told, that if ever they be heard, it fhall be after a furrender of national dignity, independence, and felf-government, and a great increafe of their paft damage, is a degree of infolence, and a contempt of juftice, rarely experienced in the annals of the world. The nation that can impofe fuch terms has no principle to reftrain it. The nation that can fubmit to them is prepared for all oppreffion.

Force only can decide between them; or the one muſt be a tyrant and the other a ſlave.

The diſpatches are in the hands of every one, and no honeſt American but muſt burn with indignation at their inſolent demand of conceſſions for the Preſident's ſpeech. Shall they impudently interfere in the diſcretionary adminiſtration of our government, not affecting them, and we not ſpeak with reſentment! Shall we pave the way to a negociation by a diſavowal of truth, and a profeſſion of falſehood! O! if they had found the envoys baſe enough to ſubmit to theſe terms, there would have been no humiliation ſo great that would not have been required of them.

But theſe were but pretexts. The real preliminary was money. Money in bribes and in gifts under the name of loans. For a loan from a weaker to a more powerful government. is but another name for a gift or tribute; eſpecially when the government requiring the money is avowed to have no regard to juſtice, is publicly compared to the Indians and Algerines, and declared like them to ſell peace and forbearance of their cruel aggreſſions. With ſuch a government having made one conceſſion, would there have been any end of demand, while we had any thing to give? Indeed, at once they avow, that their expectations are in proportion to our ability to pay. The firſt conceſſion was putting our necks under their feet. And true intereſt, as well as true dignity, required that we ſhould ſtop at the point of right.

But would it not have been better to have made this conceſſion ? By no means. When a government diſavows any regard to juſtice, declares that nothing is to be obtained from it without money ; not pretending any claim of right, like Indians and Algerines, ſets out on the principle of general plunder and exaction ; and fairly owns that her demands will be meaſured by our means of ſatisfying them ; we can never hope, by any conceſſions, to ſtop exaction, while we have any thing to give : eſpecially when the men whom we ſhould now glut with our tribute might be out of power in a few weeks, and a new ſet not leſs ravenous and more hungry than they, on new pretences, and with the ſame terrors, might demand new ſupplies. Our envoys had no aſſurance, if all the demands were complied with, how the money could be diſpoſed of, or what terms, or whether any terms of accommo- dation would be accorded to them. Nor, if they had received ſuch aſſurance, could any confidence be placed in it : for whenever in mutual tranſactions, the baſis of right, juſtice, and mutual intereſt is departed from, all confidence is gone ; the party exacting what is not founded on this baſis, becomes a knave, and if he have power, a tyrant; and the party yielding, lays himfelf at his feet, and muft fubmit to whatever is required of him. Befides, no conceffion from us can fave us from her aggref-fions, while fhe is at war with England. For it is the ruin of England that fhe feeks, and her plundering us is one of her means of accomplifhing that main object. And if we make the conceffions required, while Britain is at war with France, we fhall certainly draw on ourfelves a war with Britain.

But ftill would it not be better for us, by not re-fifting, to avoid a war with France?

What thofe men mean who, fpeaking of our prefent fituation with refpect to France, talk of avoiding war, or of keeping out of war, I have never been able to comprehend, unlefs they mean, that we ought to permit France in peace, to take all our feamen, our fhips, and our property by piece meal; unmolefted in peace, to reduce us to a ftate of ftarving beggars; and then, when we have no means of defence, if fhe think proper, to come in peace and cut our throats, parcel out our lands among her foldiers, and give up our wives and children to their lufts. This feems to be the darling peace of thofe men. No refiftance, unlefs our territory be invaded. Let France go on and take our ships, our seamen, and our wealth; it is true, that will deprive us of all means of self-defence, stop our agriculture, manufactures, and arts; but then we shall be at peace. If, indeed, France ever invade our country, then we shall go to war; and if then we be incapable of defence, and can procure neither arms, cloathing, nor provisions, we may confole ourfelves with the reflection, that we have facrificed all thefe to peace; and in peace furrender our lives, property, liberty, and independence to the French, and again fit down under the bleffings of a colonial government.

But fome may fay France is too good for us to fear any fuch fate from her. Is not this the fate that all the ftates which fhe has curfed with her protection or invafion have experienced? Has fhe not in all of them ftirred up troubles, difcontents, commotions, feditions, and infurrections, and, under the pretence of aiding, or fuppreffing, or punifhing the infurgents, reduced them to implicit fubjection to her will. What are Spain, Holland, the Italian kingdoms and republics, Switzerland, Rome, Flanders, and great part of Germany, but colonies or dominions of France, plundered of their wealth and reduced to poverty? What is Venice, a neutral nation over-run by the arms of France, received under her protection, and promifed a democratic form of government, incited to commotion reduced to the condition of a conquered country, plundered of her fleet and wealth, erafed from the lift of nations, and bartered to the Emperor. France was not too good to do all this to Venice: and this is the nation with whofe fate we are now threatened by France.

France has long been carrying on war againft us, in the fafeft and moft effectual way for her, and the moft deftructive to us; a war on her fide, and peace on ours. It is now upwards of five years fince fhe began it.—From flender beginnings, fhe has proceeded to extravagant degrees of fpolia-tion, extended the extravagance of her pretexts and plunder, according to the degree of our pa-tience. The government remonftrated; but the French government knew they dared not re-fent. They had a party among ourfelves ftrong enough to defeat all the energy of our govern-ment, and they might fafely proceed to any meafure of oppreffion. In this party they yet confide; and in this confidence threaten us not only with further plunder, but with ruin. And unlefs we fhew them by an open and unanimous approbation of the paft, and confidence in the fu-ture conduct of our adminiftration; that we are determined to fupport our government in a juft refentment, they will proceed in their fpoliation, extending the extravagance of their pretences and

their violence, as we extend our patience; till they
difable us from all means of defence, and reduce us to abfolute poverty, dependence, and fubjection.

This is the only kind of war that France can
carry on againft us, with any profpect of accomplifhing her object, and fubjecting us to her will.
While fhe continues this war, and we continue our
delufive peace, our ruin is as certain, as will be
our fecurity, if we now fix our foot and fay, *We
will yield no more.* Here we take our ftand, and
from this moment we will repel all aggreffions.
We will no longer feek fhelter under the influence
of a foreign government, but under the parental
guardianfhip of our own. And the authority of
our own government we will maintain, or perifh
with it.

But is there any hope, that we fhall fucceed in
cur refiftance? Whether there be or not, our condition can hardly be worfe. For, under the laft
decree of France, hardly any of our fhips will ef-
cape condemnation, if they choofe to take them;
and their difpofition to take them we cannot doubt.
And as their refentment is violent againft Britain,
and our deftruction would injure that nation, we
can hardly doubt that after rendering us defencelefs, they will feek to deftroy us.

But there is hope that refiftance will be fuccefsful, and obtain us peace, at leaft, if not juftice.
France has now nothing to fear, while we acquiefce
in her violence; but if we refift we may repel,
and even revenge, if not remedy it. While we can
maintain a tolerable portion of fhipping and commerce, we can obtain fuch fupplies, as will enable
us to fupport ourfelves againft an invafion, if it
fhould be attempted.—But we are at fuch a dif-
tance from France, and fuch is the crippled ftate of
her navy, that it is not likely that fhe will attempt
an invafion of us, while fhe is at war with Britain,
or if fhe do attempt it, it is not likely that it can be
fuccefsful. If there be a profpect of an European
peace, France muft depend, for her future great-
nefs, on her manufactures, commerce, and fhipping. Thefe only can make her a rival to Britain. And, to fupport thefe, fhe muft have a foreign market. America is one of the moft important markets in the world for European manufactures. If the French government find, that they
can no longer maintain their influence here, by a di-
vifion or party among the people againft the government, and find, that the people unite with
the government in juft refentment againft them
for their cruel and unprovoked aggreffions; they
muft have loft all prudence, if they do not fee that
a continuance of injury will rivet indelible preju-
dices againft them in the American mind, and

difappoint all hope of fecuring any tolerable fhare of trade with us ; and they muft have loft all regard for the future glory of their nation, and all refentment againft Britain, if they do not change their conduct towards us, and, endeavour to conciliate our affections.

On thefe grounds, it appears that France has long been carrying on an infidious and deftructive war againft us ; that fhe will continue this kind of war, in proportion to our patience and fubmiffion, until fhe has firft difabled, and then ruined and fubjected us ; that there is no other way of obtaining an end to this war, peace, and juftice, but by refiftance ; and that a ftate of refiftance to fuch war is more advantageous to us, than fubmiffion, and will be effectual to procure us peace, juftice, and national independence.

It is therefore the duty of the government, having offered all reafonable terms, and exhaufted all means of reconciliation, to prepare the nation for a ftate of felf-defence ; and to convince France, that we will no longer fubmit to unjuft depredations, and violent invafions of our rights of property and fovereignty. War is a dreadful calamity. But in felf-defence, it becomes a duty both for nations and individuals. And a government, which fuffers another government unjuftly and without refiftance, to exhauft it by plunder, and render it defencelefs, thereby to ruin and enflave it, is like a man who quietly fuffers a robber to tie his hands and bleed him to death, thereby to feize his property.

The people alfo have duties to perform. When an independent and free nation has its fovereign rights attacked, and violated by another nation ; it is a call of Providence to all the citizens to ftand forth, and defend the caufe of truth and national liberty. Union in refiftance becomes as much a duty in all the citizens, as it is the duty of all the members of a family to unite in defence of the houfe againft midnight affaffins or incendiaries. And in the difcharge of this duty, to which Providence calls them, they ought to look up with holy confidence to the protection of that Providence which calls them out to trial, and to the ftrength of the Lord of Hofts, who calls them to battle. His providence and ftrength America hath heretofore experienced : and the Lord, which delivered us out of the paw of the lion, will deliver us out of the hand of the Philiftine.

To a truft in God we ought to unite confidence .n thofe men whom Providence hath called to rule over us. We fee that the conduct of the Prefident and his council has been virtuous, liberal and enlightened ; that he has done every thing practicable

F

to avoid war; and that war is brought and continued on us, by the malice and injustice of our enemies. Those slanders with which base men have obscured the light, truth, and wisdom of our government, have been chased away like mists before the sun. Let us return therefore from our error. Let us restore to our administration that confidence which never ought to have been withdrawn. And as our enemies have taken advantage of our jealousies and suspicions of our government, and made the divisions arising from them, grounds of their presumptuous hopes of destroying us; let us remove this cause of danger, if we would avoid the danger itself. Let us shew, that the people and the government are of one heart and one mind. United we stand : divided we fall.

As, to remove danger, we must remove divisions, jealousies and suspicions, so to remove these, we must silence slanderers, and set our faces against them. We have seen the sad effects, and the gross misrepresentations of those lying newspapers, lying pamphlets, lying letters, and lying conversations, with which the country has been filled. It is no longer a season to trifle with public opinion or popular passion ; lest God give us up to strong delusion, and suffer us to fall into destruction. Let us turn a deaf ear to those lying prophets. Let us withdraw from them all belief, all aid, and all countenance. They are vipers in our bofom, vultures preying on our bowels, and fatal inftruments of the malicious pur-pofes of our enemies. No good man, with a juft regard to his own reputation, will any longer fup-port or countenance them, for, by doing fo, he gives them confidence, and enables them to be mif-chievous. Silence thofe flanderers, and we fhall be as happy as we are free, as united as we are happy, and as formidable as we are united.

Finally, in order to remove the danger thereby threatened, it is our duty to endeavour to remove that impreffion, which our divifions have made on the French government. As they reft their hopes of injuring us on the belief that there is a party among ourfelves devoted to their will; let us fhew them that there is no fuch party. Let us unite in one band of unity among ourfelves, and confidence in our adminiftration; and, to teftify this union and confidence to the world, let us unanimoufly fign an inftrument, expreffing to our government our con-fidence in the rectitude of its meafures, our firm reliance on the protection of divine Providence, for the fupport of our independence from a foreign yoke, on this as on a former occafion; and, for this fupport, now as then, pledging to each other our lives, our fortunes, and our facred honour.

FINIS.